I'M THE BIGGEST!

IN THE RIVERS

LAURA K. MURRAY

CREATIVE EDUCATION   CREATIVE PAPERBACKS

CONT

LET'S EXPLORE THE RIVERS!

Cloudy water swirls and flows downstream. Use your binoculars to watch a saltwater crocodile lurk in the water. The croc is waiting to snap up its next meal.

Flowing Lengths

Rivers flow into lakes, oceans, or other rivers. Many scientists consider Africa's Nile River (opposite) to be the longest river in the world. It stretches more than 4,200 miles (6,759 km). Montana's Roe River is much shorter. It is only 201 feet (61.3 m) long.

contiguous United States width:
approx. 2,800 miles

Nile River length: 4,200 + miles

Waterfalls form as rivers flow over rock and **erode** it. The world's highest waterfall is Angel Falls in Venezuela. It towers more than 3,200 feet (975 m) high.

Rooted by the River

Black willows and other trees near rivers have dense, shallow roots. This helps keep the trees in place. Grasses also grow along riverbanks. Their stems are hollow. Rushes and sedges are common grasslike plants. Their stems are usually solid. Many have shallow, widespread roots.

Other river life forms are much smaller. **Algae** can be too tiny to see with the naked eye. They are an important food source for animals. But too much algae is harmful.

algae - plant-like organisms that do not have stems, roots, or leaves

green algae

Animals, Big and Small

Saltwater crocodiles are found in rivers, swamps, and **estuaries** of Asia and Australia. They are the biggest living **reptiles**. They weigh up to 2,200 pounds (998 kg). They can reach 23 feet (7 m) in length. South America's green anacondas are even longer. But the snakes weigh less than crocodiles.

estuaries - areas where salt water and fresh water meet

reptiles - cold-blooded animals that usually have scales or plates

15

Many river animals live entirely underwater. Amazon river dolphins are smaller than their ocean cousins. They have longer, thinner snouts. Tiny **parasites** live off larger animals such as catfish.

parasitic worm

parasites - living things that live on or in another (called a host) for survival

Full of Life

From algae to saltwater crocodiles, rivers are full of life. What other amazing things can you discover about these flowing places?

river otter

green anaconda

piranha

redtail catfish

saltwater crocodile

20

IN THE
RIVERS

Longest on each continent:

7

Onyx River
25 miles

6

Murray River
1,558 miles

5

Volga River
2,193 miles

4

Missouri River
2,341 miles

3

Yangtze
3,950 miles

2

Amazon River
at least 4,000 miles

1

Nile River
about 4,200 miles

Word Review

Do you remember what these words mean? Look at the pictures for clues, and go back to the page where the words were defined, if you need help.

algae page 12

erode page 9

estuaries page 15

parasites page 17

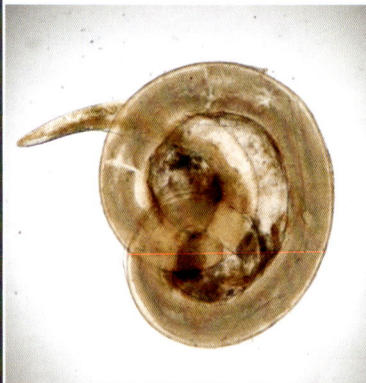

reptiles page 15

Read More

Hewitt, Sally. *Rivers*.
Mankato, Minn.: Amicus, 2011.

Manning, Paul. *Amazon River*.
Mankato, Minn.: Smart Apple Media, 2016.

Websites

Kids' Crossing: Rivers
https://eo.ucar.edu/kids/wwe/river2.htm
Check out this information about how rivers work.

World Biomes: Freshwater
http://kids.nceas.ucsb.edu/biomes/freshwater.html
Read more about the plants and animals in freshwater bodies.

Note: Every effort has been made to ensure that the websites listed above are suitable for children, that they have educational value, and that they contain no inappropriate material. However, because of the nature of the Internet, it is impossible to guarantee that these sites will remain active indefinitely or that their contents will not be altered.

Index

**PUBLISHED BY CREATIVE EDUCATION
AND CREATIVE PAPERBACKS**
P.O. Box 227, Mankato, Minnesota 56002
Creative Education and Creative Paperbacks
are imprints of The Creative Company
www.thecreativecompany.us

**LIBRARY OF CONGRESS CATALOGING-
IN-PUBLICATION DATA**
Names: Murray, Laura K., author.
Title: In the rivers / Laura K. Murray.
Series: I'm the biggest.
Summary: From shortest to longest and biggest
to smallest, this ecosystem investigation uses
varying degrees of comparison to take a closer
look at the relationships of river flora, fauna, and
landforms.

Identifiers: ISBN 978-1-64026-064-1 (hardcover)
ISBN 978-1-62832-652-9 (pbk)
ISBN 978-1-64000-180-0 (eBook)
This title has been submitted for CIP processing
under LCCN 2018938954.

CCSS: RI.1.1, 2, 4, 5, 6, 7; RI.2.1, 2, 5, 6, 7;
RI.3.1, 2, 5, 7; RF.1.1, 3, 4; RF.2.3, 4

DESIGN AND PRODUCTION
by Joe Kahnke; art direction by Rita Marshall
Printed in the United States of America

PHOTOGRAPHS by Alamy (aarrows, AfriPics
.com, Clint Farlinger, Paulo Oliveira, Travelscape
Images), FreeVectorMaps.com, Getty Images
(FEBRUARY/Moment, Maria Stenzel/National
Geographic), iStockphoto (abadonian, byllwill,
fotoslaz, Grafissimo, Jaykayl, Lana2011,
lightyear105, PhillipMinnis, roberthyrons,
rogkov, rpeters86, Sinhyu, zyxeos30), Minden
Pictures (Kevin Schafer), Shutterstock (anythings,
Choksawatdikorn, Paola Crash, Credo Graphics,
FOTOGRIN, gagolina, Eric Isselee, Dmitry
Kalinovsky, kwest, MongPro, Deiby Quintero,
Senata, sharptoyou, spline_x, yod67)

FIRST EDITION HC 9 8 7 6 5 4 3 2 1
FIRST EDITION PBK 9 8 7 6 5 4 3 2 1